Y
F
Mayer

$14.95

P9-ELO-365

DATE DUE

THE
GOLDEN
SWAN

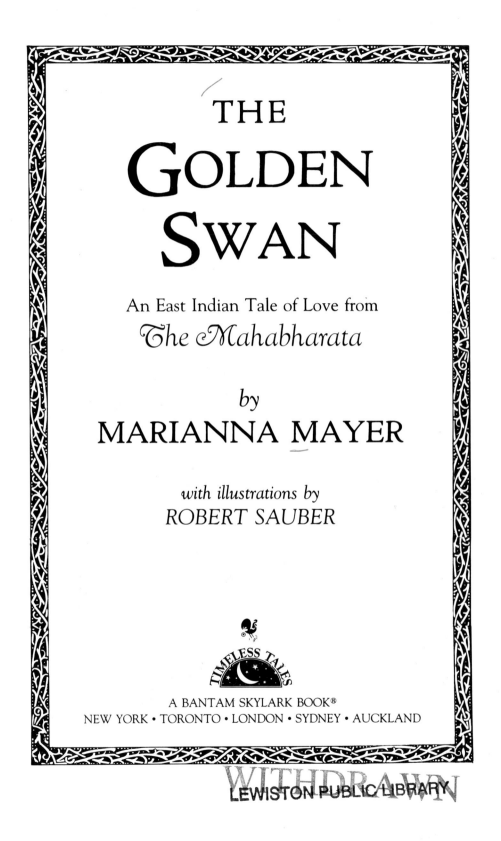

THE GOLDEN SWAN

An East Indian Tale of Love from
The Mahabharata

by

MARIANNA MAYER

with illustrations by
ROBERT SAUBER

A BANTAM SKYLARK BOOK®
NEW YORK · TORONTO · LONDON · SYDNEY · AUCKLAND

For Tom Locker

By means of the easy and the simple we grasp the
laws of the whole world. When the laws of the
whole world are grasped, therein lies perfection.

I CHING

THE BOOK OF CHANGES

THE GOLDEN SWAN

A Bantam Skylark Book / November 1990

Skylark Books is a registered trademark of Bantam Books,
a division of Bantam Doubleday Dell Publishing Group, Inc.
Registered in U.S. Patent and Trademark Office and elsewhere.

Library of Congress Cataloging-in-Publication Data

Mayer, Marianna.
    The golden swan : an East-Indian tale of love from the Mahabharata
/ by Marianna Mayer ; with illustrations by Robert Sauber.
        p.   cm.—(Timeless tales)
    "A Bantam Skylark book"—T.p. verso.
    Summary: A couple who are true mates are torn apart by a
vengeful god and suffer greatly before they find each other again.
    ISBN 0-553-07054-1
    [1. Fairy tales.   2. India—Fiction.]   I. Sauber, Robert, ill.
II. Nalopākhyāna.   English.   III. Title.   IV. Series.
PZ8.M4514Go   1990
[Fic]—dc20
                                                           90-671
                                                           CIP
                                                           AC

Published simultaneously in the United States and Canada

Bantam Books are published by Bantam Books, a division of Bantam
Doubleday Dell Publishing Group, Inc. Its trademark, consisting of the
words "Bantam Books" and the portrayal of a rooster, is Registered in U.S.
Patent and Trademark Office and in other countries. Marca Registrada.
Bantam Books, 666 Fifth Avenue, New York, New York 10103.

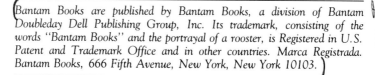

Acknowledgments

I AM GREATLY indebted to Larry DeVries, Sanskrit scholar and folklorist at the University of Chicago Library, whose guidance, assistance, and advice were so essential to my understanding the original Hindu material. Thank you to William Alspaugh, assistant to the bibliographer of the Southern Asia Collection at the University of Chicago Library, for his prompt replies and invaluable sources.

Special thanks go to Dr. Carlo Coppolo of Oakland University for the excellent comments and suggestions he offered. In addition, my gratitude to John Tillinger and Veronique Dulac for their efforts in translating a difficult French text. I would like to thank Lilli Scott for her kindness in lending skillful objectivity to this writer at the plot's earliest development.

Many thanks also to Gerald McDermott, who continues to give tirelessly of his time and talent. And finally to my editor at Bantam Books, Judy Gitenstein, who throughout this project and the others in the Timeless Tales series extended her sensitivity and support to this most grateful author.

Handwritten annotations:

Anotated Edition, 2021

Go played with Sugarloaf ◯◻◻

~~Soul life~~ gardenoteden 5.

Last month 31 years ago ~~Retire Spring~~ May

UCL 2020.

☑ sp. galiard? Ars Mysterium or library science. Diploma Holder.

◻ (Sheffiled, Amaya.)

2nd Cousin

(mcdermitt)

to the Original Irma, of Maine. Born 1940, died 1980, of Human Paploma Virus, Due to the crips Street gang. May they Burn in hell. Nice Book though

Irma Crab $plushie, pink gugley eyes. green

Preface

MY PRIMARY SOURCE and inspiration for *The Golden Swan* is the Sanskrit poem *The Mahābhārata*. The epic consists of eighteen volumes compiled from 400 B.C.–A.D. 400 and framed by a story involving the saga of five exiled, royal, and heroic brothers. The side stories, or episodes within the collection, include legends, romances, theology, and ethical as well as metaphysical doctrine. More than any other text in Indian civilization this remarkable treasure trove is a veritable storehouse of ancient Hindu lore. As with many other epics of this type, we must look upon this vast work as something akin to a library contributed to by many tellers rather than as a single literary composition.

Within the third volume, entitled *The Book of the Forest*, I first discovered the story of Nala and Damayantī, perfect mates drawn together by one of the golden swans called *hamsa*, emissaries of the gods, and subsequently tragically separated by the fatal throw of three dice, which reappear in the guise of three white birds called *sakuna*.

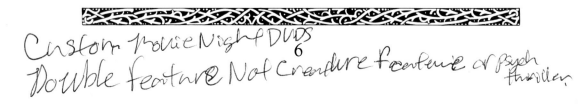

Custom Movie Night DVDS
Double feature Not Creature feature or Psych thriller

After *The Bhagavadgītā,* which can also be found within the pages of this remarkable epic, this is the best-known Indian tale in the West. Its popularity in India is attested to by the many versions it has inspired. I also found numerous folk versions separate from *The Mahābhārata,* particularly in northern India. There it is historically documented that Nala became king in A.D. 295, and he is recorded as responsible for founding Nawār in Rājasthān.

Beginning in India as early as the twelfth century and later spreading to the West as recently as the twentieth, artists have been fascinated with this poignant tale of love in separation. Operas have been composed on the theme, and it has inspired romances, poems, and plays both in our language and in many others.

Nala and Damayantī's story is strikingly different in spirit from the other episodes in its celebration of womankind. Though there is no proof that it was originally written by a woman, it is fair to assume that it was written *for* women. Even today, songs praising Damayantī's enduring love are sung to young brides on their wedding day.

The line between the gods and mortal men in Hindu myth is most intriguing, for it is tissue-thin if not wholly nonexistent. Mortals can achieve divine power and even divinity in a variety of ways, while the gods in India are most human in their whims and desires. Less than godly acts might result

7

in casting a god in the form of a mortal for several lifetimes until he redeems himself. In the same manner, the gods often attempt to keep man firmly in his place, that is to say, mortal and earthbound. Not wanting competition, they think nothing of throwing obstacles and temptation in the path of a mortal whose character might otherwise win him or her a place as a deity.

Indeed, the gods involve themselves intimately in the affairs of men on earth, rescuing a favorite or causing utmost havoc. In all ways they indulge themselves and turn the road leading from heaven to earth into a highly traveled path.

Clearly such activities are in evidence in the story of Nala. Kali, the god of misfortune (an ancient deity now totally usurped by the later medieval goddess named Kālī), is key to mastering the twists of fate that are dealt to Nala. Kali is the very essence of the worst throw of the dice—snake eyes, or bad luck.

Here I set the task to create a fresh tale, motivated by these elements but not rigidly based on material of the past. Instead, all the stories in the Timeless Tales series are original, using old tradition as their source of inspiration. For this reason *The Golden Swan* and the other tales in this series should be read not as works of scholarship or adaptation but as works of pure imagination.

MARIANNA MAYER

Chapter One

HERE ONCE LIVED a king named Nala. He was strong and handsome, an expert with horses, renowned for his mastery over fire, but some said too fond of games of chance.

Nala was king of the Nishada people. As a warrior he was unequaled. His palace was famed for its splendor, and all who entered his realm were welcomed. One fine summer evening a band of traveling minstrels came through, and the king invited them to entertain him.

When the minstrels began to play, their music delighted Nala. The melodies spun pictures in his mind. One song after the other told story after story, and it was nearly dawn before the musicians stopped to rest.

Finally, the last song began and it was the most enchanting of all. The lyrics spoke of a certain princess; Damayanti was her name. From birth she was favored with such extraordinary beauty that it was said that she had been made from the grains of loveliness gathered from everything beautiful in the

world. Nala, who had never found a woman he could love, listened, spellbound. The music wove a gossamer web to bind him, and within its soft, melodic sound a clear image of the princess appeared to him. Then and there, Nala's heart was pierced by love for Damayanti.

When the song was ended, the minstrels collected their instruments and went on their way. But the vision of Damayanti lingered. Indeed, Nala found he could think of little else. Love's golden arrow had made him sick with longing. He yearned to meet her, though he knew that this would be no easy task. Damayanti lived far away, and until it came time for her to marry, the princess would remain in seclusion, as was the custom. Nala prayed that the fates would be kind and allow him a means to meet her before she wed another.

The next morning, in the palace garden, Nala saw a flock of golden swans with red-tipped wings circling above him. Slowly the flock descended until at last they alighted on the waters of a large pool in the garden. The king crept to the edge of the still water, and though the swans rose to fly away, he caught the most beautiful of all.

The captive looked beseechingly into Nala's amber eyes and said, "King, let me go free. If you do, I will fly to the distant kingdom of Vidarbha where the princess Damayanti lives. I know that it is there that your heart resides. Trust me to advise

the princess that she should marry only you. For you see, dear Nala, the wind and the clouds, the sea and the sun have told me that this is your destiny. You, Nala, shall never love another."

Amazed, Nala released the golden swan. Immediately the bird flew off to join his companions. Days later the flock arrived in Vidarbha where Damayanti sat among her young friends. The girls marveled at the golden swans as they landed. They hoped to tame them, but try as the young women might to catch the swans, they could not. Instead, the birds led the maidens off in different directions. One particular swan gave Damayanti a merry chase this way and that till the princess was far from her friends. Suddenly, in the spreading shade of a tall, graceful willow tree, the swan turned and faced her. Without moving, he allowed her to draw closer. Slowly she reached out to stroke the swan's long graceful neck. In the shadows his feathers looked like spun gold, and the tips of his wings were as red as blood.

"Glorious creature," whispered the princess, "you are so very beautiful."

The swan turned to gaze at her fully. "Thank you, gentle maiden," he answered. "You should know that I have flown far and wide and seen many sights strange and wonderful, but never have I seen a woman whose beauty could equal yours. You are like a golden swan yourself, for you are as rare among your kind as I am among mine."

Damayanti laughed softly and her cheeks turned crimson at the pretty compliment. "You say this only to be polite."

But the swan tossed his head, saying, "No, princess, it is not always polite to state what is true. Besides, I know only too well that to be made beautiful is of no great benefit. Dear princess, I fear that like me your beauty will bring you no happiness, unless you find the one mate in all the world who can love you for yourself.

"Wherever I go there are those who wish to capture me. They wish to make me *their* prize. But what right do they have to me? I belong only to my own chosen mate. She is everything I could wish. I know she was created for me as I was for her. If I were to lose her, I would die of loneliness. Should you meet your true mate, it will be the same for you. Of this I am certain."

"Ah, swan!" exclaimed the princess with tears in her eyes. "What you say moves me beyond words. In my heart I know this to be true. Tell me, please, you, who have seen the world and love so completely, do you know of one who could be such a mate for me? I long to love someone as you describe."

"Yes, but only one man, princess," replied the golden swan. "His name is Nala and he is a king. Nala is the only mate for you. Out of the thousands upon thousands of kings and princes I have seen, he alone can give meaning and happiness to your life.

But who can say if he will ever marry. You see, princess, he waits for you."

That evening, Damayanti went to her father, King Bhima, and told him that she was ready to choose a husband. Her father was delighted, and he hastened to arrange for every eligible king from far and wide to come to his great city to vie for the princess's hand in marriage. But it was made clear that the invitation called for a *swayamvara,* and at such a ceremony it would be the princess Damayanti who would do the choosing and no one else.

Chapter Two

FF IN THE HEAVENS four gods had heard of the *swayamvara*. They knew well of the princess Damayanti's rare beauty. Indeed, they believed she had been set apart from ordinary women, for she bore a birthmark upon her brow that shone like the sun. Each god wanted her for his own. They were Indra, the storm god who was fair and loving; Agni, the brilliant fire god; Varuna, the powerful lord of the seas and rivers; and Yama, the dark though gentle god of the dead.

In a golden chariot the four gods descended toward earth to present themselves at the princess's choosing ceremony. As they traveled, Indra spied Nala, who was also on his way to Vidarbha. The celestial companions stopped and made themselves visible.

The storm god spoke first. "I am Indra, and with me are Agni, Varuna, and Yama. We wish you to deliver a message to the princess Damayanti if you are going in that direction."

Nala bowed to the gods and answered, "I am.

But King Bhima keeps his beautiful daughter well guarded. It is unlikely that I will see her before the appointed hour for all hopeful suitors."

Indra gave a wise smile and said, "But *you* will see her. And when you do, tell the princess that we four are coming to her choosing ceremony so that she may choose a god for her husband."

"I will do as you ask. No matter how difficult," replied Nala.

Then Indra bent down and took up a bit of dust from the road. He sprinkled this over Nala, saying, "This will make your task far easier than you suppose, good king. At midnight go into the palace, and you shall find the princess without peril."

When Nala looked up, the gods were gone.

On the following day, as Nala drew near Vidarbha, he ordered his royal caravans to go on to the great city without him. In light of the gods' request he believed he should enter the city alone and on foot.

At sunset on the same day Nala entered the city gates. The streets were dusty and crowded with all kinds of people. Wanderers and vagrants, royalty and entertainers, farmers and tradesmen, their friends and families all came to witness the choice of the princess Damayanti, known to be the most beautiful princess ever born. Meanwhile, unencumbered, Nala easily passed through the noisy city without attracting the least attention.

Nightfall found him standing in the deep shadows of the high, white-walled palace. Beyond the fortress the air was cool. Nala could smell the jasmine blossoms and the black aloewood trees in the royal garden. He heard the soft sound of lute music and saw the gleam of gold and silver from within the pearl-white pavilions where a sumptuous supper was being served to the new arrivals. Silently Nala waited for the stroke of twelve.

At midnight he entered the palace, walking past King Bhima's guards without question. Not a soul saw him. No one barred his way, for Indra had made him invisible to all who might have stopped

him. As though guided, Nala found his way into Damayanti's private rooms. The princess was with her attendants, who were busy adding the final touches to her wedding gown.

At the sound of footsteps all the young women looked up. Nala stood before them. Startled, they stopped what they were doing and stared at him in wonder. Each thought, He is so handsome! He must be a god! But which one is he?

At the sight of him Damayanti's heart began to race, and all at once she felt such love for this handsome stranger. But he was no stranger to her. Indeed, somehow she felt as though she knew him.

"Welcome, lord," she said. "What is your name and how did you find your way here?"

"Princess, I am Nala. Indra has sent me with a message for you. It is thanks to him that I have managed to come here unseen."

Of course Damayanti recognized Nala's name. The words of the golden swan came back to her. Now she truly understood what the bird had told her. "Majesty, please sit beside me and say what you will."

Nala did as she asked. He was moved beyond measure to be at last in her presence, but his mood was solemn. He must carry out the duty the gods had entrusted to him, though he wished nothing more than to profess his *own* love for her.

"I must keep my word to the gods," he began.

"I bring you a message. Four gods will come to your choosing ceremony. Each hopes you will pick him for your husband."

"Thank you, I will remember," replied Damayanti with a faint smile, for she felt she could read Nala's thoughts. Hoping to draw him out, she asked, "And Nala, will *you* attend?"

"Yes, princess. Even before the gods asked me to be their messenger, I traveled here for that sole purpose."

For a moment Damayanti could do nothing more than look back into Nala's steady gaze. She wished for him to stay, but fearing for his safety, she said instead, "Now we must say good night. You are in grave danger so long as you remain. We shall meet again."

Chapter Three

T THE APPOINTED hour the next morning, one by one the magnificent assembly of suitors filed into the great hall to take their places and await the arrival of the princess. Restless, they eyed one another jealously and seemed for all the world more like an unruly herd of wild and fiery-eyed stallions than an assembly of kings.

The tension mounted as the minutes passed. The rival kings shifted in their seats and trained their eyes on the door through which the princess would enter. Just then the door opened, and the princess, carrying the garland of white lotus blossoms she would give to her chosen mate, entered. A hush fell across the assembly as she walked to her seat beside her father. Watching her, the hopeful suitors had only one thought: The princess Damayanti with her golden skin and rich black hair was more exquisite than any king ever imagined.

The princess sat perfectly still, her pale blue eyes were cast down as the name of each king present was called. When this was done, there was

silence. Every king held his breath as he waited to see which one of them Damayanti would choose.

She rose and carried the garland to Nala. But there before her sat not one, but five young men identical to Nala in every way.

Tricky gods, thought Damayanti. So you know I wish only to make Nala my husband. Well, you will not fool me.

"Stand up, Nala," she said aloud.

All five young men stood up at once. Carefully, Damayanti studied each one. She saw that four pairs of eyes stared straight at her but did not blink, and four pairs of feet did not touch the floor. Inwardly the princess smiled. She placed the garland of flowers around the neck of the true Nala to acknowledge her choice.

Tenderly, Nala took her hand in his, saying, "I will always love you. Nothing shall ever part us."

Indra whispered to the other three gods, "This is well done. Damayanti has made a true choice. Let us concede our loss and remove our disguises."

In an instant, all four gods vanished.

"Alas, we have not won her," said all the other kings, and then they, too, left for their own kingdoms.

As the gods made their ascent back to the heavens, they encountered Kali, the snake-eyed god of misfortune.

"Where are you going in such a hurry?" asked Indra.

"I am off to seek the princess Damayanti," answered Kali. "I have decided to take her as my wife."

"You cannot," Indra said firmly. "Damayanti has already chosen. She and Nala have exchanged vows. You must leave them in peace."

Kali narrowed his slanted green eyes and said, "Since Nala has been chosen over the gods, I will curse him."

Indra pointed to his quiver of thunderbolts, and his voice grew deep and threatening. "It was done well, Kali. They go with my blessing. Do not test my patience. If you curse Nala with doom, I will see that you are punished."

The gods left Kali, but no warning could suppress his jealousy. Secretly he went in search of the loving couple.

Chapter Four

ITH THE WEDDING celebration at an end, Nala and Damayanti said farewell to her father. The road to Nala's own kingdom was taken at a leisurely pace. At times they sent their caravans on without them so that they could walk hand in hand alone.

One day they came upon the seashore, blue-green and fresh smelling; it seemed to go on forever. "It's like my love for you," Nala told her. "Never ending and always full."

That evening, under a luminous moon, they slept beside a quiet lake, where, in deep silence, animals came to drink. Then, in the heat of the following day, they found a dark, cool cave hidden far from all the world. There they held each other close and whispered secrets they had never thought to share before.

Alone as they were, without a care but for each other, Damayanti grew even more beautiful. Nala thought her a treasure worth more than any kingdom or the earth or himself.

But even at this pace, they soon reached

Nishada, and there they took up a new life together. It was here that Kali found them. The sight of their happiness drove him into an even fiercer rage. Burning with malice, he went to Nala's brother, Pushkara, and said, "I am going to possess Nala and destroy him. Come and throw dice with him. You, who have never won against him, now cannot lose."

Pushkara needed no further persuasion. Weak-willed and jealous by nature, he also envied Nala for his kindness and his wealth, and most of all for his beautiful wife, who had eyes for no one but her husband. So he did not hesitate. Instead, he hurried to challenge Nala to a game of dice that by the strict rules of honor could not be refused.

But Pushkara came in the guise of a loving brother. He brought with him marriage gifts for Damayanti. There were golden chests filled with silver and leopards with diamond collars and white horses with ruby bridles.

"May your union grow and prosper like a tree with deep, strong roots. May it never falter. May it never fail," was Pushkara's blessing for them.

At twilight that evening Damayanti was left as the brothers began to play against each other. Hour after hour passed and Damayanti grew worried. She went to Nala and gently touched his sleeve, begging him to be cautious. But he did not hear her. He had already begun to lose, and Kali's power was consuming him.

Day by day, little by little, at each throw of the dice he gambled away all he owned. Failing to persuade him on her own, Damayanti then sought friends and relatives to urge him to stop. But Nala remained deaf to their pleas. Soon they left him, saying to her, "The Nala we knew is lost. We must forget him and so must you."

At last only Damayanti remained to look on helplessly as her beloved Nala was stripped of everything.

Finally, Pushkara said, "You have nothing more to wager. Unless you wish to play for your last and rarest treasure—Damayanti herself."

At the sound of Damayanti's name Nala seemed to come to his senses for a moment. Rising, he flung his royal robes to the floor without a word and turned away. Damayanti walked with him as he left the palace; each wore only the simple robe of a beggar. It was all they had now to call their own, besides each other.

Chapter Five

OMELESS AND PENNILESS, they drifted. Pushkara was now king, and his first royal order was to command that no one give shelter or aid to the former king Nala under penalty of death. For three nights the couple slept on the ground on ther outskirts of the city where once they had reigned as king and queen. Then, with nowhere else to go, they entered the forest. There they lived on fruit from the trees and bitter roots pulled from the earth. But they were always wary, for the forest was a deadly place filled with wild beasts and demons.

Then, one day Nala thought his luck had changed, for he came upon three birds. Cautiously he took off his single robe and threw it over one, hoping to capture it for Damayanti's supper. In a flash the birds flew up, carrying away the flimsy garment. One bird called back, "We are the three dice you threw to lose all. We did not wish to leave even one single piece of cloth with such a fool."

Humiliated, Nala turned to Damayanti and spoke in a strangely unfamiliar voice. "See ahead,

where the roads cross. The right path will lead you back to your own homeland. Leave me and follow it."

"Don't even suggest it! I can bear anything but that we should part," said Damayanti, and her eyes filled with tears.

Nala shook his head, trying to make sense of his thoughts, and when he answered his voice was his own again. "No, you are right," he said. "I would sooner die than lose you."

"But we can go to Vidarbha together," suggested Damayanti gently. "I know my father would welcome us."

Nala shook his head. "Once you could be proud of me. Now I can only bring you dishonor. I must remain here, hidden from the world, until this misfortune is lifted."

That evening they discovered a shelter, a small wooden hut in the midst of the forest. They thought it strange to find such a place in the wilderness, but they entered, grateful for the hope of protection. Weary from the long day's journey, Damayanti was soon sound asleep. But Nala could find no rest; his mind was filled with conflicting thoughts.

All day long a voice kept insisting that he leave Damayanti. Now in the darkness he listened miserably as it continued.

"If you leave her, she will return to her father. There she will be safe. Soon enough she will forget all about you and be happy again."

The voice was Kali's. His vengeful power was growing ever steadily, consuming Nala by the hour. Nala did not know it; he believed it was reason speaking, urging him to think only of Damayanti. The cunning Kali was using Nala's great love for her against them both. With such a weapon he could not fail.

All at once Nala rose up and left Damayanti. It was the hardest thing he had ever done. As he walked off into the shadows, he tried not to look back. But, then, after a step or two, his resolve failed him, and he turned to look at her sleeping figure.

The sight of her lying there so delicate and trusting filled him with tenderness. He could not leave her. With all his heart he longed to return and rest by her side. Yet the voice would not stop.

"Leave her!" it commanded. *"You are no longer the hero who deserves such a woman."*

Nala tried not to listen. Returning to the hut he told himself, "I will die without her."

The voice laughed. *"Weak-willed Nala! What earthly good are you to her? Penniless, destitute, all you can do now is cling to this defenseless woman. What can you give her but disgrace. If you were any man at all you would leave her."*

In the darkness a battle between love and reason waged within Nala. Again he left the hut. But he felt torn in two, held fast by his love and driven

away by the deceptive reasoning that compelled him to go. His heart was breaking.

In the struggle Nala's will was shattered, and with this came another change. For the weaker Nala grew the stronger Kali became. Finally, Nala left for the last time. He ran into the darkness, his heart pounding, his face bathed in tears. But the man who ran from the hut no longer resembled Nala. For Kali's evil magic had transformed not only his mind but his body as well. Gradually, almost imperceptibly at first, the fine features in Nala's handsome face melted and became distorted.

With every step away from Damayanti, the change became more complete. His long legs grew short and thick. His broad, muscular shoulders sagged. His straight back bent, and in seconds a ghastly hump appeared. Indeed, the pale, dwarfish figure that now moved off into the desolate night seemed more animal than human. The royal hero, King Nala, had ceased to exist.

It was a master stroke for Kali to transform Nala. Clearly he could have stopped there and rejoiced over his triumph. But Kali was still not satisfied. He wished to wipe out all trace of Nala and the sweet memory of his love for Damayanti. So with one last act of revenge he let a veil of forgetfulness fall over Nala's mind.

"Soon," whispered Kali, *"you will be a forgotten man even to yourself."*

Chapter Six

T FIRST LIGHT, Damayanti opened her eyes to find Nala gone. Thinking that he could not be far, she began to call him. But when there was no reply she grew anxious.

Where could he have gone? she wondered. But when she saw no sign of him, she became truly desperate and she cried out, "How long can you survive without me to love and care for you? Is it so easy for you to leave me?"

Still there was no answer. In the silence of the forest she began to feel real fear, not for her safety but for his. Not knowing where to look for him, she ran in one direction then another, calling, searching. Her long black hair fell loose as she ran, tangling with stray branches and broken blossoms. Sharp thorns snared her thin robe and tore her bare arms and legs. Heedless, she ran on, her mind fixed only on Nala.

The day passed and she did not find him. Yet she still could not believe he had left her. Toward late afternoon the light in the forest faded, and in

the deep shadow she was forced to turn back. Exhausted and bleeding, she returned to the shelter.

All through the lonely night she huddled in a small corner of the hut and listened for every sound, hoping it was Nala at last. Indeed, the night seemed an eternity of waiting.

Dawn found her drained of hope. Surely now there was no point in waiting any longer. She rose up, dry-eyed, and told herself, When he first threw the dice it seemed a madness had overtaken him. But nothing can make me believe that Nala left me of his own free will.

With her fist raised to the heavens she called out, "In the name of the gods who saw me choose Nala as my mate, hear me. May the one who brought this misery down upon us one day be punished and receive greater pain than ours." With this curse still on her lips, she left the shelter uncertain of where to turn next.

Off in the heavens Indra heard Damayanti's words. He had watched with dismay Nala's battle between love and madness. Angry, Indra rolled his thunderclouds down over the blue mountains to the forest far below. Wrapped in a cloak of mist and rain, he bent close to the earth and whispered to his great friend the serpent king. Silently his friend listened. At last the serpent answered, "It shall be done."

Chapter Seven

N THE DAYS that followed Nala slept little, encountering no one. Instead he drifted aimlessly; all that had gone before was now a blank to him. The memory of his beloved Damayanti was forgotten.

Then, one early dawn before the sun spread through the forest, Nala found his path cut off by a wall of flames. Filled with curiosity, he moved nearer. Clearly this was no natural forest fire. The high flames gave off no heat, burning nothing, not tree, vine, or tender blade of grass. The blaze was wholly contained, a tall, strangely cool column of white fire, raging endlessly.

As he stared hypnotized by the flickering light, Nala heard a voice from amidst the flames call to him.

"Come! Come closer. Have no fear," said the voice. "I am the serpent king, Karkotaka. I am trapped here in the flames. But you can free me. You can carry me away. The fire will not harm you. See for yourself. Here, step in and pick me up. I will make myself as tiny as your little finger. For

this kindness, I swear I will be your friend and give you something that will profit you."

Nala could not resist. He stepped forward and the flames parted, making a clear path for him to enter. At the same time the huge serpent grew smaller and smaller until he was no bigger than a tiny ribbon snake one might find in a garden. Amazed, Nala picked him up and walked out of the flames unharmed.

When they had gone a safe distance, Nala attempted to set the snake down. But Karkotaka said, "Wait a moment longer. Walk a little farther. Count your steps and I shall tell you when to stop."

Nala went on, counting as he walked, and on the tenth step the snake bit him on the left wrist. Startled, Nala dropped the snake.

In the next instant the snake resumed his former size. Rising to his full height, he towered over Nala. "Believe me," said Karkotaka, "I mean you no harm. Instead, I have done you a good deed, even if you doubt it. You see, the great god Indra sent me to aid you."

"What need have I of your help?" asked Nala as he rubbed the spot where he had been bit. Curiously the serpent had left no mark and there was no pain.

"So then it is true, you have no memory of your past misfortune."

Nala frowned and shook his head; no, he did not remember.

The serpent was silent for a few moments and his flashing emerald eyes changed to deep turquoise then yellow and again to emerald green before he spoke once more. "What then do you call yourself?"

Again Nala shook his head; he did not remember his name.

The serpent sighed. It was not difficult to see what Kali had done to Nala.

"Listen, friend," the serpent continued, "and I shall try to explain. Without your knowledge you have acquired a most powerful enemy. My venom should weaken his hold on you and cause him no end of pain.

"But you must do as I tell you. Leave the forest and seek the realm of King Rituparna. Tell him you wish to train his horses. With your great skill he will gladly welcome you, for he is in need of a master charioteer."

Then the serpent pointed to a white silk robe which lay folded neatly at Nala's feet where an instant earlier there had been nothing. "When you wish to resume your true form, put this robe on and think of me. Now go to King Rituparna. You shall see, he will be a good friend to you."

Chapter Eight

AT DAWN A delicate mist still lingered over the small lake where Damayanti had come to fall asleep. Now sunlight warmed her face, and she opened her eyes to find the wild wood filled with the singing of birds and the buzzing of insects. She washed in the cool lake water and left the clearing.

Her wanderings took her past moss-covered hills and rushing silver streams. Bears and leopards, lions and deer concealed by the lush greenery lining the path paused to watch her. Yet Damayanti saw none of this, so intent was she on thoughts of Nala. Clearly she was not aware of the tiger drinking at the edge of the stream until she was far too close to escape him. But through her sorrow she had lost her sense of fear.

"Mighty tiger," she began with a solemn bow, "I am searching for my mate. He is Nala, a hero in his own time and once a great king. Have you seen him?"

The tiger slowly blinked his bright yellow eyes and stared at her. Long ago his kind had lost any

interest in speaking to people. And yet something in Damayanti's quietly determined manner caused him to pause.

Still he said nothing, and she was left to wonder if in the next instant this fiercest of creatures might choose to strike and devour her.

"I cannot say that I have seen such a man," said the tiger at last. "But if he is your mate, that is to say your *true* mate, surely he would not have left you."

Fresh tears welled up in Damayanti's eyes, and

she lowered her head. "I cannot explain his reason. I only know that he is my true mate. Even if I never see him again, I am bound to him now and forever."

"Such love is noble, child," said the tiger, and he pitied her. "But of little comfort to one so young. Tell me, though. What will you do should you find him?"

"I shall take care of him," answered Damayanti. "With all my heart that is what I long to do."

"Perhaps his misfortune causes him to believe he is in little need of that. Or he may think he is not deserving of such love as yours. Remember, child, each soul's journey is his own." The tiger was quiet for a moment before continuing. "But if he is your true mate, your paths will cross again. Of this I am certain."

"Then I shall help him see that he is worthy as all are worthy of love."

At sunset Damayanti came before a scarlet-blossomed asoka tree. She knew its name meant *no sadness*. She walked around it three times, as was the custom when seeking good omens, before asking for news of Nala. "My marriage bed was adorned with your sweet red blooms. And yet, I have lost my mate. Why were we not blessed with happiness?"

The asoka's leaves trembled as a soft evening breeze passed through the forest. The last rays of sunlight filtered through the branches of the tall tree, making its bright blossoms seem aflame.

"There are forces stronger than mine," answered the asoka tree in a whisper. "And not all of them for the good. But you may still know happiness."

"Only if you can tell me where I may find Nala."

"This I cannot do, for he has not crossed my way, child. You must seek him elsewhere."

That night Damayanti slept at the foot of the white mountains. At dawn she awoke to find a garland of scarlet asoka blossoms about her neck. She brushed the paper-thin blooms against her lips, releasing a blood-red liquid from the bruised petals. The juice was bitter on her tongue and stained her lips.

In late morning Damayanti spied a tranquil hollow, still and green beyond the footpath. Three hermits made their home there, living on water, air, and fallen leaves. They had come as young men, and they had grown old and wise while seeking truth. Round them the antelope, wolf, and rabbit played together with other animals, trusting in one another and in man. Trees laden with fruit and flowers grew by a flowing river where silverfish darted and jumped, tame yet free.

Unwilling to disturb such a peaceful scene, Damayanti hung back, watching in awe. But one of the ancient ascetics with a bird resting on each shoulder saw her. Beckoning to her, he said, "Here, now, lovely one. Don't be afraid. You are welcome. Come and sit awhile with us."

"It is a good life you have here among the trees and the animals. It is a life most serene."

"Yes," answered the ancient. "But not for everyone. Tell us, who are you and what has brought you to us? Your beauty brings to mind the goddess of the forest. Is that who you are? But you look so sad. Tell us why."

"I am Damayanti, searching the whole forest for Nala."

"Then go to Vidarbha and wait."

"No. That is where he will never be."

"Trust us, dear princess," said the ancient. "Return to your father. You will never find your mate this way. But you will see him again."

Damayanti's eyes filled with tears, and she covered her face with her hands. She longed to believe these words to be true. When she looked up again the tiny hermitage had vanished, and nothing—not river, animal, or men—remained. The color left Damayanti's face. Now she stood up, knowing what she must do.

It was the next day that Damayanti, lean and wild-looking, was met on the roadside by a caravan of merchants. They willingly allowed her to join them, and in several days she was in her father's great city again. But she could not bring herself to enter the palace. For three days she wandered the streets like a beggar, when at last, Sudeva, one of the king's holy men, chanced to see her.

"Why do you walk through your city like a stranger?" asked Sudeva. When she didn't answer, he rubbed the dust from her forehead, revealing her birthmark. "Your brilliance is like the sun covered by a storm cloud. Your Highness, your father has sought you everywhere. Why are you hiding from those who love you and wish to help you?"

"I am searching for my heart that is lost."

"Your father's heart is also lost. If you love your father, go to him. Let him send his best men to find Nala for you."

"Yes," said Damayanti. "I cannot find him alone."

King Bhima had many loyal men with sharp eyes and ears in his service, but among the royal court there were no men the king valued more highly than his wise ones, the brahmins as they were called. Sudeva was one, but there were others.

Once Damayanti was restored to her family, her father told her, "Let me send my brahmins in disguise across the length of the land in search of Nala. But you, child, must tell me what you wish them to ask."

"Say this," answered Damayanti. " *'Beloved gambler, where have you gone? You who are so kind, why are you unkind to the one who loves you most?'* "

Chapter Nine

HEN THE DWARFED Nala reached Rituparna's kingdom, he told the king, "Take me into your service, Majesty. I will gladly train your horses so that they shall fly like the wind."

"Then stay with me, friend," answered the king. "Be my master charioteer and teach my horses all you know. I will reward you with anything you wish."

Months later, a brahmin weary from traveling settled in the stables to take shelter for the night. Nala gave him food and drink. In return the stranger whose name was Parnada told him, "In a dream I heard a question, and since that day I can think of nothing else."

"What is the question?"

"Listen and I shall repeat it. *'Beloved gambler, where have you gone? You who are so kind, why are you unkind to the one who loves you most?'* "

Nala's eyes filled with tears. Shaking his head, he looked away and said, "These words could mean anything. But it might be the cry of a woman who

was abandoned somewhere. Perhaps in a forest. If so, can there be any doubt that she is dead by now. You must put it out of your mind. It will do you no good to think of it."

"But surely she must still be alive."

"Friend, how long was it that you had this dream?"

"No more than two months ago."

"That gambler could be waiting for something, you know. If she could still love him after everything he's done . . ." Nala stopped speaking as he considered his words. "But, no," he continued. "How could she love someone so weak that even birds can steal the last bit of what he owned?"

Not more than a week later, Parnada, who was in truth one of King Bhima's brahmins, stood before Damayanti. "Searching for Nala, I finally came to the domain of King Rituparna. I spoke your words a thousand times to anyone who had ears to listen. Never did I receive a reply that led me to suspect there was even one who knew of Nala.

"But then, in the king's own stable, a dwarf, misshapen and bent as if under some evil star, answered me. And though ugly, he spoke like a king.

"On the following morning, while he still thought me asleep, he prepared our morning meal. At his touch, suddenly the straw burst into flame. As though this were not proof enough of his mas-

tery over fire, I then watched him assemble the burning logs with his bare hands. With my own eyes I saw that although his hands should not have withstood the flames, *they were never burned*! I swear to you, Your Highness, that by his appearance he could never be mistaken for Nala, and yet it can be no one else."

Damayanti breathed a sigh of relief. "Blessed Parnada, I only pray that what you say is so. But I beg you let this be our secret for a little longer."

When Parnada agreed, Damayanti called the Brahmin Sudeva to her. "Listen, friend," said Damayanti, "for I must ask a great favor. Ride to King Rituparna's kingdom without delay. Tell him that you are my father's messenger come to announce that I intend to choose another husband on the very next day at the rising of the sun."

As soon as Rituparna heard the news, he ran to the stables, looking for his master charioteer. "There is not a moment to spare!" said the king when he found the dwarf. "You must get me to Vidarbha tonight! If you can, I'll give you whatever you desire."

Pacing, the king anxiously pleaded that they be off at once, but Nala would not be rushed. Instead, he selected his horses with the utmost care. At last, four long-legged animals with powerfully broad chests and bold hearts were chosen. As Nala harnessed them, he stroked their long necks and

whispered in their ears. Satisfied, he took up the reins.

"Are you sure we can manage this long journey with only four horses?" asked the king, as he hastened to get into the chariot.

"If you don't trust my judgment, Majesty, please take more."

"No, no," insisted the king. "Pay no attention to me. Of course, I leave it all to you. Only please, get me there quickly."

"And so I shall!" said Nala as he called to his horses.

Suddenly all four horses sprang forward, and in the next instant they leapt up and flew into the sky. The chariot was pulled up higher and higher, streaking through the clouds toward Vidarbha as if it were an arrow shot from a mighty bow.

The wind was in the king's hair, and his heart was racing with excitement as he looked down. Trees and land flashed by; never had he imagined such speed was possible except in his most fabulous dreams.

Above the roar of the wind, he shouted to his master charioteer, "You are a wonder! A genius with horses as I am with numbers!"

"How is that?" asked Nala, halting the chariot in midair.

"Well, I shall show you," said the king, and looking about him for an example, his eyes alighted

upon a tree. "See down below? There is a nut tree my people call the dice tree, for it is from such trees that dice are made."

"Yes," remarked Nala, "I see. What of it, Majesty?"

"Now," continued the king, "you will witness my remarkable skill at counting. With one glance I can tell you that the difference between the leaves and the nuts still on the tree and those fallen on the ground is a hundred and one—one more leaf and one hundred more nuts. What is more, by exact count there are fifty-one million leaves and two thousand ninety-nine nuts on the tree.

"Wait!" said the king with alarm. "Why are we going down?"

"What you say amazes me! I must find out if your count is right or wrong."

"*What!*" exclaimed the king, incredulous. "There is no time for that!"

"I must," insisted Nala. "You can leave me here and take the horses to Vidarbha yourself if you cannot wait. But I must know if your count is correct."

In moments the chariot had descended, and Nala leapt out.

"Master Charioteer," urged the king in a soothing voice, "please, no one else can drive these horses but *you*. I will never reach Vidarbha by sunrise unless you take me. Count if you must. But *please* hurry!"

Nala counted every leaf and nut both on the tree and on the ground. Astonished, he found that the king's numbers were precisely correct.

"This is a wonder beyond wonders, Majesty! I see you are a genius, indeed. I must know the magic of your talent. Teach me, I beg you."

The king, who was in a great hurry to be off, reluctantly replied, "You should know that my knowledge extends to the secret of dice as well as counting. But, Master Charioteer, there is no time to learn such things now."

"Give me that magic lore and in return I will not only get you to Vidarbha on time, but I will also teach you my secret with horses."

"Will you really do both these things for me?" asked the king.

"I swear it!" answered Nala.

The king knew well enough that he had already promised whatever his master charioteer desired, and he dearly wished to understand the secrets of horsemanship. So he agreed.

At the moment that Nala received the secret of the dice from the king, Kali's power was at an end. Retching the poisonous venom that the serpent king had used against him, the defeated god materialized before Nala.

To all else, Kali was invisible, and yet Nala saw him quite plainly. The fire of Kali's curse was dispelled and Nala was free. Slowly, like a veil

being drawn back, Nala's memory returned to him. But he was ravaged, worn thin by the pain and anguish Kali had caused him. Now, seeing his enemy filled him with rage, and a curse formed upon his lips.

Frightened and trembling, Kali fell to his knees and implored Nala, "Please, I beg you to have mercy. I have suffered enough from Damayanti's curse. It is because of her that Indra told the serpent king to poison me. I swear, I am defeated, and you need fear no danger from me. I will never do you harm again."

Nala did not doubt these words. His anger dissolved and he turned away. Seeing his opportunity for escape, Kali quickly entered the dice tree. Nala was never to see him again.

Chapter Ten

OOD AS HIS WORD, Nala took his horses up into the sky again, and the chariot flew to Vidarbha. When they arrived King Rituparna saw at once that there were certainly no preparations for a *swayamvara*. Masking his embarrassment and surprise, he cordially greeted King Bhima.

"For what do we deserve such a rare honor?" inquired Bhima.

Rituparna thought for a moment before answering. Finally, smiling warmly, he said, "Too long I have wanted to pay my sincere respects to you, Your Royal Highness. I hope I am welcome."

"Welcome? I am overjoyed by your visit!"

Even though King Bhima imagined quite rightly that there was more to this visit than was being explained, he was delighted to welcome Rituparna, whom he admired greatly.

Soon Rituparna was ushered into the palace, and the master charioteer was sent to the royal stables to unharness the horses. All this Damayanti watched from her balcony. Now, shaking her head,

she withdrew into the privacy of her rooms. It cannot be, and yet my heart assures me that this dwarf is Nala, she told herself. Who else could have driven these horses here at such speed?

Presently she slipped away from the palace and entered the stables where the dwarf was seeing to his horses.

"It would appear that you have traveled a long way in a very short time," said Damayanti. "Tell me, for what reason did your king visit us?"

Nala could not look her in the eye, but he forced himself to answer, "King Rituparna wished to be present at your choosing ceremony, Your Highness."

"I wonder, Master Charioteer," remarked Damayanti, "have you heard the sad tale of the man who deserted his wife in the forest as she slept? A man, I might add, who made a vow to her, saying, *'Nothing shall ever part us'*?"

"I have," replied Nala, but Damayanti had to strain to hear him, for his words were barely a whisper. "And so," he continued, "since the madman did this, how could anyone blame the woman for finally choosing another husband. Even if that wretch were still alive, unknown to anyone but himself. Surely he has no claim to her love."

"He is known, Majesty," answered Damayanti. "Nala, there is no *swayamvara*. My dearest love, why is it that you still hide from me?"

In a broken voice Nala asked, "How is it that *you* could still love Nala?"

"Even in death I shall love you, for you are my true mate as I will always be yours," she told him.

"He has wronged you and is not deserving of your love."

"He is wrong only in not forgiving himself."

Nala reached under his shirt and drew out the white silk garment the serpent king had given him. "Go now. Walk to the palace. I shall follow after you in a moment."

When Nala caught up with Damayanti, he took her hand in his. She saw that once more he was in body and soul the man she knew. The past was nothing now but a dark night lit by the burning flame of their everlasting love.

Chapter Eleven

HE NEXT MORNING Rituparna and Nala clasped hands. "To think that you were my master charioteer! If I have done you any injustice, I beg your forgiveness."

"You have only done me the greatest good, friend. And now I must say farewell, for I am bound for my own kingdom of Nishada, where I must settle a score."

With Damayanti at his side Nala returned to his kingdom. Pushkara came to the gate himself when he saw his brother approaching.

"What do you want here?" asked Pushkara.

"I give you a challenge," said Nala. "Come and throw dice with me."

"What do you have to wager, brother? Well," said Pushkara with a rueful laugh, "it makes no difference. Since you've been gone, I have had no fun playing dice with anyone. Come, we shall play. I will stake everything I won from you against Damayanti. Lose and she shall wait upon me for the rest of her days."

"Let us begin, at once."

Each threw the dice. In one single throw, Nala won back all he had lost. His kingdom and his life were once again restored to him.

Never again were Nala and Damayanti to be parted. Happiness was to follow them through their long, full life together. But when they breathed their last breath, they were put to rest in a single grave, and from that spot an asoka tree soon took root. Its scarlet blossoms, more vibrant than most, drew loving couples from far and wide. As was the custom of old, each couple circled the tree three times and gathered the blooms for their marriage bed, hoping for happiness and perhaps not knowing that sometimes true love may be as bitter as it is sweet.